Murder beneath the Ballroom Chandelier

A Little Firling Mystery – Book Three

by Belinda Chavremootoo

Dedication

For every cat who ever solved a mystery

quietly before the humans caught up.

About the Author

Belinda writes charming cozy mysteries filled with seaside secrets, garden gates, and cats who always know the truth. When not plotting fictional crimes, she can be found in her own garden where the earthy scent of soil and the gentle rustle of leaves provide inspiration. Her two cats supervising everything with quiet judgment.

Coming Soon: Murder between Brushstrokes

A Little Firling Mystery – Book Four

Annabel and Evie's art retreat turns chaotic with the sudden disappearance of famous artist Elena Halberd. As they delve into the mystery, they uncover secrets—chasing a stolen brooch, missing sketchbooks, and a cryptic note hinting at stolen creativity. Hidden rivalries and tensions surface. With Persephone the cat by their side, each clue brings them closer to a perilous truth, exposing the dark side of artistic genius.

Table of Contents

Prologue

Little Firling had never needed help keeping secrets.

They lived in the stone of the old mill, nestled beneath rose trellises, tucked into second scones at the Hare & Hound. And when those secrets grew too heavy to bear, they tended to slip — through misplaced letters, forgotten heirlooms, or the occasional suspicious death.

In her short time living there, Annabel Lennox Deighton, retired literature professor and recent transplant from Glasgow, had already uncovered more mysteries than most villagers experienced in a lifetime. With her sharp mind, a well-worn notebook, and a cat who refused to be left out of anything, she'd solved a death on the cliffs and uncovered long-buried treasure.

But the past never stays buried for long in Little Firling.

Now, spring has brought flowers, festivities... and a gala that will end with a glittering crash.

Because in Little Firling, murder blooms when no one's looking.

And Persephone is always watching.

Chapter 1

It was the kind of evening that dared you to blink.

Lanterns glowed like suspended stars above the gardens of Everly House, and inside, the ballroom shimmered under the weight of a thousand reflections. Gilded mirrors. Polished marble. Sequins. Ambition.

The scent of cut lilies mingled with beeswax polish and something faintly metallic — the smell of money, secrets, and heirlooms that had been fought over in court. Velvet drapes muffled laughter and gossip into a kind of conspiratorial hush, like the walls themselves were in attendance, listening closely.

The strings played soft and slow — the sort of music designed to make you feel wealthy, even if you weren't. The chandeliers twinkled like they were in on a secret. And the champagne? Breathtakingly dry and impossible to hold on an empty stomach.

Annabel Lennox Deighton sipped hers anyway. Annabel had once lectured on Shakespearean tragedy at the University of Glasgow — a career marked by sharp analysis, dry wit, and a faculty nickname that translated roughly to "the velvet scalpel." Retirement hadn't dulled her instincts. If anything, Little Firling's quiet veneer offered new stagecraft for her mind: smaller dramas, tighter scripts, but just as much blood beneath the surface.

She stood near the edge of the ballroom, one eyebrow arched at a topiary that had been shaped, inexplicably, into a swan wearing a powdered wig. A nod to the Versailles theme of the gala, she supposed, though she'd seen fewer wigs and more weaponised gossip.

"If this is meant to be Versailles," she murmured, "they've taken creative liberties."

"Darling," said Evie Barnes, appearing at her elbow, "they're nobles. Creative liberties are a lifestyle."

Evie had been raised in the village — or more precisely, rescued by it. Her aunt, the late Constance Caldwell, had taken her in from the orphanage when she was six and raised her above the village bookshop with stern affection and endless paperbacks. Evie commuted regularly to Surrey to work as a journalist, sharp-eyed and sharper-tongued, before staying after her aunt's passing. She now ran the bookshop — and a running commentary on village life — with dry humour that sometimes masked her wariness. She didn't make friends easily. Annabel had recognised that immediately. And then made herself the exception.

Their invitation had arrived through a combination of favours and horticulture — Annabel had recently helped re-catalogue the Everly House archive for a family legacy exhibit, and the Little Firling Garden Society had contributed to the event's flamboyant theme. It had been meant as a community showcase. The Everly family had turned it into theatre.

Which is how two clever women — and one very particular Bombay cat — ended up drinking champagne beneath a chandelier while surrounded by powdered wigs, faux French accents, and social tension so thick it needed carving knives.

Persephone, of course, had not been invited. She had simply arrived — as she always did when something terrible was about to happen.

At present, she lounged near the base of the dais, watching the room with narrowed eyes and that particularly regal contempt reserved for murder suspects and people who used synthetic lavender.

Annabel hadn't taken the archival work out of boredom — not quite.

It had begun with a polite letter from Lady Vera, a nudge from the Garden Society, and maybe a whispered memory of her late husband, Michael, lingering in the corners of her old study.

She hadn't been looking for work.

But after decades of teaching, her mind still paced like it needed something to solve. Vera's invitation had come with flattery and veiled expectations — "You're sharp, Deighton. You see through things. I need that."

The job hadn't paid, not in anything that mattered.

But it gave her keys to the Everly library.

Access to Vera's "legacy drawers."

And perhaps, just perhaps, one last puzzle worth solving.

She hadn't expected that puzzle to come with champagne, powdered wigs, and an impending corpse.

Which is why, when Lady Vera Everly swept into the room ten minutes late — all black velvet and pearls, flanked by gossip and disdain — Annabel watched her very, very carefully.

She'd seen enough in the Everly archives these past weeks — edited letters, charred corners, one curiously unsigned envelope — to know that Vera was planning something.

And when Lady Vera planned, people usually ended up furious, disinherited, or both.

Vera made her usual orbit, declined several toasts, made a single withering comment about a duchess's choice of brooch, and settled beneath the chandelier in a chair no one else dared claim.

She lifted her gin fizz.

And then she stopped moving.

***

One day earlier. Late evening. Everly House, Drawing Room.

Vera stood at the window, her silhouette outlined by firelight. The glass of port in her hand trembled — not from age, but from decision.

Clarissa Fairmont entered without knocking. She had once played Lady Macbeth in Stratford and never quite stepped out of character. She and Vera had shared a long, thorny friendship — part loyalty, part performance.

"You rang like a monarch. I assumed it was either treason or tea."

Vera didn't turn. "You're still here."

"I never leave before the curtain falls."

A pause.

"I'm changing the will," Vera said.

Clarissa inhaled sharply but kept her voice cool. "To Juliet?"

"To justice."

She turned, eyes gleaming like storm clouds.

"You always wanted the spotlight, Clarissa. But you never wanted the weight of it."

Clarissa's voice cracked. "You're doing this because I loved you."

"No. I'm doing this because I finally love myself enough to stop hiding."

Vera approached, placing a velvet pouch on the mantle.

"They're yours. For now. Keep them safe."

Clarissa didn't move.

"What if this goes badly?"

"It already has."

***

At first, it didn't look like anything at all.

Just Vera. Being still. Judging. Uninterested.

But Annabel's eyes were sharper than most. And she saw it.

The hand that didn't tremble. The glass that didn't tilt. The pearls — missing.

Evie was the first to speak. "Annabel."

"I see her."

"Is she—"

"Yes."

And that was when the screaming started.

Persephone stood.

Tail high. Ears alert.

She turned once, slowly, toward Annabel — and blinked.

We begin.

Chapter 2

The ballroom had shifted.

The glitter still sparkled; the strings still played — but now everything moved like it was underwater. Slower. Sharper. As if the murder had soaked into the walls and no one wanted to touch anything too hard.

Lady Vera lay still beneath a crisp linen cloth, draped hastily by a horrified footman. Her drink had been removed. Her chair had not.

Annabel stood nearby, watching the ripples.

People whispered. Gestured. Avoided looking directly at the body.

It wasn't grief. Not really. It was something more brittle, more self-conscious. Like embarrassment at the disruption of a well-planned evening.

Clarissa Fairmont lingered near the French doors — once Vera's closest friend, now the faded shadow in her mirror.

A woman in pink tulle nearly dropped her champagne. A footman caught it mid-fall, eyes wide.

"More like social self-preservation," Annabel murmured.

Evie handed her a fresh champagne flute and shrugged. "Dead duchess at a Versailles ball. Bit on the nose, really."

PC Tom Oakes had arrived — flustered, sweaty, and brandishing a notepad like it might defend him from the nobility. PC Oakes had been posted to Little Firling a couple of years ago after an unfortunate incident involving a lost swan and a broken antique vase in Devon. He was still recovering his dignity.

He approached with the puffed-up earnestness of someone very much out of his depth.

"Miss Deighton," he said, trying for authoritative. "If I could ask for your discretion—"

"Of course," Annabel said calmly, cutting him off with a smile sharp enough to slice a vol-au-vent. "You'll want names, movements, points of tension?"

Oakes blinked. "Well, I suppose, yes—"

"She was dead before dessert," Annabel continued. "Her posture never shifted. And she didn't touch her drink once."

She handed him a cocktail napkin with names scrawled in elegant script. "Start there."

Oakes stared at it like it had sprouted claws. Nodded dumbly. Shuffled away.

Evie sipped. "I love when you go full professor."

Annabel scanned the crowd, eyes sharpening.

Rafe Everly, the nephew — investment banker, professional eldest son — stood near the orchestra, face taut, tie askew. He wasn't looking at the body. He was looking at the solicitor, Mr. Grantham — and whatever they were saying, it wasn't condolences. Mr. Grantham, the family solicitor, had been with the Everlys for nearly three decades — discreet, precise, and famously unbribable. Or so he liked to say.

"Rafe was furious at dinner," Annabel said quietly. "She toasted Juliet instead of him. It wasn't subtle."

"Neither was that snub at the heritage fund speech," Evie added. "She all but called him irrelevant."

"Perhaps he agreed."

Seraphina May, the art dealer — all cheekbones and curated charm — who once sold a Rothko to a duchess and a forgery to her dog, if rumour was to be believed — hovered by the staircase, speaking softly to two gallery patrons. She wore sequins like armour, and her smile was one shade too bright.

Annabel tilted her head. "She was Vera's 'special consultant,' yes?"

Evie snorted. "If you mean she helped launder emotions through curated canvases, then yes."

In the far corner, Juliet Everly stood alone — Vera's niece, quiet and elegant, long presumed ornamental. But not tonight.

Hands clasped. Expression unreadable.

She hadn't cried.

She hadn't moved.

Annabel's gaze lingered.

"She's hiding something."

"She always is," Evie replied. "But this time, it might be her moment."

Mrs. Gilchrist, the Everly housekeeper, swept past them with a tray she didn't need to be holding. Her face was unreadable. Her spine was military-grade.

"Her tea has never been poisoned," Evie whispered. "But if it ever is, she'll administer it herself."

And somewhere, winding quietly between ankles and furniture, Persephone moved like smoke. Watching. Listening.

Not leading.

Not yet.

Just listening. She absorbed the room, one blink at a time.

Annabel turned her gaze to the chandelier.

"No sign of struggle. No spilled drink. The pearls are gone. And so is the will."

Evie blinked. "The will?"

Annabel smiled faintly. "Oh, there's always a will, darling."

Chapter 3

The drawing room had been sealed, though the seal consisted of a single velvet rope and PC Oakes looking embarrassed.

Annabel stepped over both with ease, her presence both unassuming and undeniable.

Evie followed, offering the constable a nod that suggested he ought to be taking notes from her instead.

The room still smelled of lemon polish and tension. Mahogany gleamed, velvet drapes muffled the light, and everything had been arranged just so — as if Vera might still sweep in and reorder it herself.

This had been her sanctuary. Her throne room. Where decisions were made, gossip curated, threats whispered with clipped precision.

It was where Vera had held court, made pronouncements, and destroyed at least three marriages — two of them with only her eyebrows.

And now, it was too quiet — the kind of quiet that made you lean in, expecting something to shatter.

Annabel crossed to the writing desk and began to rifle — delicately, precisely. Not rummaging. Investigating.

"Look for what's missing," she said.

"You mean besides the gin fizz and her pulse?" Evie replied, flipping open a drawer in the side cabinet.

Annabel gave her a dry smile.

There was something intimate in this search — not invasive, not exactly. But it was a kind of mourning. Annabel had always believed that the way a person kept their desk was the truest biography.

Vera's told a story of control, elegance, and the meticulous fear of being forgotten.

The drawers were tidy — too tidy. A sort of museum cleanliness that suggested preparation, or concealment.

She moved to the bookcase.e

Titles were arranged by genre, then author. A few volumes had been recently disturbed. A missing volume left a noticeable gap.

"Vera was exacting," Annabel murmured. "She wouldn't leave a gap."

Evie joined her, scanning the shelves.

"It's odd," she whispered. "No dust ring where the missing book was."

Annabel nodded. "Because it wasn't removed in a panic. Someone knew they were taking it — and planned for no trace."

Persephone hopped onto the piano bench and stared at the wall across from the fireplace.

Three minutes later, she meowed.

Annabel turned, following the cat's gaze.

Then frowned.

She stepped forward, fingers brushing against the painted panel.

Evie trailed her with curiosity.

The panel was subtly ajar.

Behind it — a hollow.

Inside, nestled in dust and velvet, a thin length of silk ribbon.

Annabel plucked it out and examined the faint imprint on the velvet.

"Pearls were here," she murmured. "Recently removed."

Evie knelt beside the panel. "And someone left in a hurry. That's a scuff."

She pointed to a faint mark in the wood — just barely visible where a shoe had dragged in haste.

Annabel tucked the ribbon into her notebook and glanced back at the empty velvet hollow.

"Why hide them here?"

Evie shrugged. "Why not a safe?"

"She wanted someone to find them. But not just anyone."

She touched the inside of the panel once more. The velvet was worn smooth. This hadn't been hidden recently — it had been used before.

Annabel turned to Persephone.

"Well spotted."

The cat blinked once.

A flick of her tail.

Of course.

Chapter 4

Clarissa Fairmont hadn't left the premises.

Which was a shame, really, because she had the air of someone who might confess to murder just for the drama of it. She wore black silk, had reapplied her lipstick with theatrical precision, and was presently holding court in the Everly library with three guests who hadn't yet realised the gala was definitively over.

When Annabel entered, Clarissa gave a tiny, amused smile, as if they were about to embark on an interview for the society pages rather than an informal inquiry into murder.

"I suppose you've come to ask me uncomfortable questions," she said, folding her legs elegantly.

"Yes," Annabel replied. "But I imagine you're more likely to volunteer something unhelpful."

Clarissa laughed, delighted.

"You know, I always liked you, Deighton. You're the only one who doesn't pretend to find me mysterious."

"Your opinion of me is inversely proportional to your standing with Vera."

Clarissa's smile froze for half a second. It was a good freeze — almost imperceptible — but it was there.

"I didn't kill her."

"No," Annabel agreed. "But you might know who wanted to."

Clarissa dropped into a chair with the theatrical grace of someone auditioning for a role no one had written.

"She changed the will," she said with a flourish. "Or was about to."

Annabel tilted her head slightly.

"She told you?"

"She told everyone — in her own way. That little speech about fresh starts. It was a warning wrapped in a toast. And Juliet looked positively seasick."

"To whom was she warning?"

Clarissa gave her a long, considering look.

"Anyone who depended on her. Financially. Socially. Emotionally."

Annabel leaned forward.

"And what were you, Clarissa?"

Clarissa's eyes glittered.

"Replaceable."

A pause.

Then, without ceremony, Persephone leapt into her lap.

Clarissa looked down at the cat, startled. "Even you, darling?"

Persephone blinked slowly.

Judgmentally.

Clarissa sighed.

"She said she was tying up the past. Getting her legacy in order. It frightened her, but she was determined."

Annabel watched her carefully.

"And the pearls?"

Clarissa hesitated.

"She had them. Said they belonged to the Everly matriarch — something about justice and shame. She didn't say more."

"And now they're missing."

Clarissa looked away.

"She wouldn't have misplaced them."

"No," Annabel said, rising. "But she might have baited a trap with them."

Chapter 5

Juliet Everly was not easy to corner.

But Annabel had spent a career coaxing revelations from students who thought silence was armour. And Juliet — with her stiff shoulders and distant gaze — was just another soul trying not to bleed.

Annabel found her in the conservatory, standing among orchids and moonlight. The air smelled faintly of jasmine, though something metallic lingered beneath it — a reminder that somewhere nearby, the house still carried the scent of death.

Juliet didn't turn when Annabel entered.

"Beautiful, aren't they?" Annabel said, stepping quietly beside her.

Juliet's voice was flat. "They're finicky."

"So was Vera."

Juliet's hands were clasped behind her back, white at the knuckles.

"She said she was tired of games. That she wanted to set things right."

"Did she say what that meant?"

"She said Rafe would understand."

"Did he?"

"She didn't get the chance to tell him."

Annabel waited.

Juliet turned slightly, face pale and composed.

"She told me she wanted to give me the gallery. Officially. Backed with trust funds and the deed to the east wing."

"That's generous."

"She said it was overdue."

"Was Rafe aware?"

Juliet's lips twitched into a tight smile.

"He's always aware."

Annabel looked at her carefully.

"She was going to name you her heir."

Juliet's composure cracked — a brief tremble in the corners of her mouth.

"I didn't want it. Not really. But I didn't want Hale to get it either."

Annabel stilled.

"Hale?"

"She never said it directly. But she kept alluding to someone — someone with long reach. Someone who could undo everything with a whisper."

"Rupert Hale," Annabel said quietly.

Juliet nodded.

"She said she was ready to stop being afraid."

"And then she died."

Juliet looked down.

"There was a man at the gala I didn't recognize. He was dressed as catering. Spilled champagne on her during the toast."

Annabel's pulse quickened.

"She reacted?"

"She looked at him like she'd seen a ghost. She didn't say anything. Just... stared."

"Did you tell anyone?"

"I thought it was nothing."

Annabel's voice softened. "And now?"

Juliet finally met her eyes.

"Now I think it was everything."

Chapter 6

The gardens behind Everly House had emptied, though the lanterns still burned as if reluctant to admit the party was over.

Annabel walked slowly along the path between the rose bushes, Persephone trotting ahead with the silent confidence of a queen inspecting her realm.

Evie joined her, carrying two lukewarm cups of tea and a new rumour about the duchess's second husband and a crate of missing champagne.

"I swear, this place breeds scandal like other towns grow tomatoes."

Annabel accepted the tea and nodded at Persephone, who had stopped beneath the ancient sundial near the herbaceous border.

She was staring at the base, tail twitching.

"Looks like we've got something," Annabel said.

Evie peered closer.

"A clue or a vole?"

Annabel crouched and ran her fingers along the edge of the sundial's stone base. It wobbled slightly.

Evie joined her, and together they shifted it aside.

Beneath, a hollow cavity.

Inside — a small velvet pouch, and a folded note, yellowed with time.

Annabel opened the note carefully.

It was written in Vera's hand. Sharp, angular, deliberate.

A diagram. A family tree. Circled names. And beneath it, one line in all capital letters:

"THE RING AND THE KEY."

Evie opened the pouch.

Inside: a signet ring bearing the Everly crest. And a small iron key, delicate and old.

"A key to what?" Evie whispered.

Annabel stood slowly.

"Something Vera didn't want Hale to find."

Evie paled. "So, it's true. She was going to expose him."

Annabel nodded. "She left breadcrumbs. This is one of them."

Persephone brushed against Annabel's leg, purring faintly.

"She always knew where to look," Annabel said.

"Cats or Vera?"

"Both."

Evie pocketed the key.

Annabel refolded the note.

And somewhere, beyond the hedgerows, the wind shifted — as if the garden itself exhaled.

***

The Hare & Hound pub smelled of cinnamon scones, wood polish, and smugness the morning after the gala.

Annabel and Evie slid into their usual booth near the window, where the light caught the flecks in Persephone's fur as she perched on the backrest, disdainful of the village chatter—but definitely listening.

"I give it till the end of the teapot," Evie muttered, "before someone casually drops a murder theory."

She was wrong.

It took exactly *three* sips of tea.

"That chandelier was never bolted in properly," said Mrs. Elspeth Muir, voice hushed but theatrically so. "I told my Harold when they hung it—'That thing's a death wish in crystals.'"

"It didn't fall, Elspeth," snapped Mr. Dunning from the fireplace. "She was poisoned. I saw her turn blue."

"Pearls were cursed," mumbled someone behind the scone display.

Annabel sipped her tea without looking up. "They've made it to the curse theory already. Impressive."

Evie leaned over. "Ten pence says we get a ghost rumour before the bill."

From the corner, young Maisie Fry—home from university and armed with a new fringe and a criminology minor—piped up: "I heard Juliet stood to inherit everything. And Rafe was *furious.* He knocked over an entire brandy tower!"

"She's not wrong," murmured Evie. "Brandy fountain *was* a casualty."

Mrs. Potts, the baker's wife, popped her head in. "And don't forget about the caterer boy. Not one of ours. Outsider. Said he 'forgot' the caviar. Suspicious, that."

"Probably Hale's doing," said someone ominously.

Persephone flicked her tail.

Annabel's eyes scanned the room. The village had absorbed the scandal the way it did all things — through crumbs, cough drops, and a barely suppressed appetite for mischief.

"Think they'll solve it for us?" Evie asked.

"No," Annabel said, standing. "But they might scare the killer into rushing."

Chapter 7

Ginny Pearce had been crying.

Not the wild, wailing kind, but the quiet, brimming sort that made her eyes red and her voice thready. She sat on a low bench near the back corridor, twisting a tissue into damp spirals.

Annabel approached slowly, with Evie just behind, holding a paper bag that contained, inexplicably, three scones and a half-empty thermos of mint tea.

"Ginny," Annabel said softly.

The girl looked up, startled. "Miss Deighton."

"You knew Lady Vera well?"

Ginny nodded, wiping her nose.

"She was... complicated. But kind. She paid for my evening courses. Said I had better things to do than polish silver."

"Did she confide in you?"

Ginny hesitated.

"She was tense, lately. Said people were watching her. That she didn't feel safe."

"Did she say who?"

"No. Just... she looked over her shoulder more than usual."

Evie handed her the thermos.

"She mention Rupert Hale?"

Ginny blinked. "Only once. She said he took what didn't belong to him and called it charity."

Annabel exchanged a glance with Evie.

"Did she give you anything?"

Ginny bit her lip.

"She gave me a letter. Said if anything happened to her, I should post it. But I... I lost it."

Evie tensed. "You lost a deathbed confession?"

Ginny shook her head quickly and fumbled through her handbag.

From a side pocket, she pulled out a small envelope.

"I never posted it. I couldn't decide if it was real or just... one of her moods."

Annabel took the envelope gently.

Addressed in Vera's looping script:

Mr. R.L. Grantham — Private & Confidential

Unsealed.

Inside: a second note. Longer. Typed. Signed in ink.

Annabel skimmed it. Then read it again, slower.

Her expression hardened.

"She names Hale. The pearls. The forgeries. Says she was ready to come forward."

Ginny looked miserable.

"I'm sorry. I didn't know it mattered."

Annabel folded the note.

"It matters now."

Chapter 8

Clarissa Fairmont was packing.

Not in a rush, not in a panic — but with a sort of tired grace, as if leaving had always been the plan, and she'd only been waiting for the right cue. Her travel case, monogrammed and well-worn, sat open on the chaise lounge. Silk scarves, leather-bound books, and one curious-looking opera mask were already tucked inside.

Annabel stepped into the room without knocking.

"You don't strike me as someone who flees."

Clarissa didn't look up. "I don't flee. I reposition."

Evie leaned against the doorframe. "Convenient timing, though."

Clarissa sighed and turned to face them. Her eyes were clearer than before. Sadder, too.

"She asked me to hold the pearls."

That got Annabel's full attention.

"She trusted you?"

Clarissa gave a rueful smile. "I was the distraction. She wanted someone obvious to take the fall if things went wrong."

"Did they?"

"I left my clutch on the sideboard during the third toast. When I went back, it was unlatched. The pearls were gone."

"Who knew you had them?"

Clarissa shrugged. "Anyone watching closely."

Evie frowned. "And what did she say when you told her?"

Clarissa's smile faded.

"I never got the chance."

Annabel moved closer.

"She planned to name Juliet her heir. The diagram in the garden hollow confirms it."

Clarissa nodded. "She thought Juliet had backbone. Said she was tired of men who mistook silence for strength."

"And you left that diagram out," Annabel said softly. "Where anyone could find it."

Clarissa stiffened. "I thought it would push her to act. I didn't mean—"

"But someone else acted first."

Persephone slinked into the room, her paws silent on the carpet.

She jumped onto the windowsill, curled her tail around her feet, and stared at Clarissa.

Not with scorn.

With pity.

Clarissa sat down slowly.

"I just wanted her to make good on her promises."

"She did," Annabel said. "In the end. But now it's our job to finish what she started."

Clarissa met her eyes.

And nodded.

***

The humans were loud.

They always were when one of them stopped breathing. Voices cracked, cups rattled, shoes squeaked. They filled the air with nonsense—fear, guilt, theories—none of it useful.

Persephone moved like smoke.

Under chairs, past spilt champagne, across marble that still carried the echo of Lady Vera's last steps.

She paused at the foot of the dais.

Sniffed.

Dust, gin, lavender, and...

Blood? No. Not fresh. Older. Faint. From behind the panelling.

She flicked her tail once.

Turned.

Out through the ballroom, past the frightened feet of a constable who reeked of biscuit crumbs and desperation.

The library was cooler.

Calmer.

She leapt silently onto the sideboard and stared at the fireplace. There it was again. The smell of silk and betrayal. The faint trace of Clarissa's perfume mixed with guilt.

But no danger.

Not *yet.*

She prowled to the piano bench. Sat. Waited.

It would come. It always did.

Persephone didn't solve murders.

She simply watched until the truth walked in.

And then she blinked.

Once.

Slowly.

The signal.

Let the clever one figure it out.

Chapter 9

The piano bench creaked as Annabel lifted the lid.

Inside: sheet music — mostly Debussy and Chopin — a small cloth pouch, and something wrapped tightly in navy velvet.

The faint scent of old perfume and varnish rose like a ghost.

Evie reached for it but paused, eyeing Annabel.

"Do we unwrap cursed objects before or after lunch?"

Annabel smiled faintly and unfolded the cloth.

A silver case rested inside. Rectangular, engraved with the Everly crest, and old enough to hum with secrets.

The metal was cool. Heavy. The sort of object that remembered being passed hand to hand in hushed rooms.

Evie raised an eyebrow. "Vera's private collection?"

"Let's see."

Annabel flipped open the case.

Inside: microfilm.

Evie leaned in. "Now we've gone Cold War."

Annabel carefully lifted the reel and held it up to the light.

"The labels match Everly estate appraisals. These are valuations — some of them altered. Others forged."

Evie exhaled. "So, she really had evidence."

Annabel nodded slowly. "And she'd begun gathering it. Methodically. Deliberately."

Her pulse picked up. Vera hadn't just been bitter — she'd been *preparing.* This wasn't paranoia. This was insurance.

She reached into the piano bench again and removed a note — a second one, folded neatly beneath the velvet.

It was short. One sentence, handwritten:

"He took what was mine. I'll take back what was stolen."

Evie frowned.

"Was she referring to Hale?"

Annabel was quiet for a moment.

The note felt colder than the case. Final. As if written by someone who'd already set the dominoes in motion.

"She must have known he'd retaliate."

"Then why do it?"

"She was tired. Of being manipulated. Of watching her family used."

Annabel looked up.

"She was preparing to fight back."

A sound behind them made them turn.

PC Oakes appeared at the door, a smear of pastry sugar on his sleeve and a very nervous expression on his face.

"Miss Deighton?"

"Yes?"

"There's someone asking for you. Says he was part of the catering team last night."

Annabel's eyes narrowed.

"Did you get a name?"

Oakes checked his notepad.

"Liam. Liam Harrow."

Evie straightened.

"Well, well. Let's go meet the champagne-spiller."

Chapter 10

Liam Harrow looked exactly like someone who wanted to disappear — thin, pale, and dressed in a jacket one size too big for his frame. His hands twisted together in his lap, and his eyes darted toward every window like they were escape routes.

The air in the parlour was still, but tense — like the room had paused to eavesdrop. Dust motes swirled in the afternoon light, ignoring the drama entirely.

Annabel studied him from across the room.

"You were at the gala."

Liam nodded.

"I was with the catering team. Plume Events."

Evie frowned. "We've checked — they don't exist."

"They don't," Liam said quickly. "I mean, they do. But not legally. I was picked up in a van with a sticker slapped on it. No ID. No names."

Annabel leaned forward.

"You spilled something on Lady Vera."

Liam swallowed.

"She brushed past me. I didn't mean to. She... she froze. Looked at me like I'd stabbed her."

"Did she say anything?"

"She said 'You.' Just that. And then she turned away."

His voice trembled on the word. Not theatrically — just enough to crack the air.

Evie crossed her arms.

"Who hired you?"

"I don't know. I got a text. Said it was a private job. Paid double in cash. Instructions were minimal. Wear black. Serve drinks. Keep quiet."

Annabel tilted her head.

"Did anyone else interact with you?"

"A man in a dark coat met me at the van. He gave me the uniform. Said I wasn't to speak unless spoken to. That's it."

Evie's voice dropped.

"You know who sent him."

"I think so."

Annabel gave him a long look.

"Rupert Hale."

Liam flinched.

"I don't know him. I swear. But people talk. And the man I saw at the back of the house when I left? That was him. Watching."

The name sat in the room like a shadow that refused to leave.

Annabel glanced at Evie.

"He's tying up loose ends."

Evie took a step forward.

"You're lucky Vera didn't scream. You'd be the body, not her."

Liam looked like he might cry.

"I didn't hurt her. I didn't even know who she was until the next morning. Please — I didn't do anything."

Annabel nodded.

"But you were a message."

Liam buried his face in his hands.

And outside, in the hallway, Persephone sat beside the door.

Waiting.

Listening.

As always.

Chapter 11

Seraphina May's gallery suite was as dramatically curated as her reputation — all exposed beams, soft lighting, and walls of minimalist paintings that cost more than an average holiday home.

She greeted Annabel and Evie in a robe of midnight silk, cigarette holder in one hand, disdain in the other.

"I assume you're not here to browse," she said, gliding toward them.

"No," Annabel replied. "We're here to discuss Vera. And the forged appraisals."

Seraphina's jaw tensed — just a flicker.

"I don't deal in forgeries."

"But you deal in acquisitions," Evie said. "And a lot of those pieces came through Everly channels."

Seraphina smiled thinly.

"Lady Vera was... eclectic in her tastes. She liked danger with her art."

Annabel stepped closer.

"She trusted you. She named you as her art advisor. That's more than taste."

Seraphina sighed and stubbed out her cigarette.

"She knew. About the pieces. Some were clean. Others... less so."

"Who pushed the dirty ones through?"

Seraphina hesitated.

"Hale. He owns part of the London gallery. Silent partner. Untraceable."

"And Vera found out?"

"She found out years ago. But she stayed quiet. Until recently. She said she wanted her legacy to be clean."

Annabel nodded slowly.

"She left evidence."

Seraphina's eyes widened.

"The microfilm."

"She hid it in the piano bench. Along with a note. She planned to expose everything."

Seraphina's face crumpled slightly.

"She said it would destroy me. And save Juliet."

Evie stepped forward.

"And the pearls?"

"I never saw them. But she talked about them. Said they were the key to realising something deeper. Family honour. Guilt. Justice."

"She baited the trap," Annabel murmured.

"And someone took it."

Persephone padded into the room.

Seraphina looked down at her.

"She never liked me."

Persephone blinked.

Then, slowly, hopped onto the windowsill — and curled up.

Observing with that particular disinterest that only cats — and very old souls — can manage.

Chapter 12

Mr. Grantham, the family solicitor, sat stiffly in the Everly study, his spine perfectly straight, hands folded atop a stack of manila files. He looked like a man who had spent a lifetime arranging secrets into tidy columns — and had just discovered one of them was missing.

The study smelled of old books and guarded silences. Sunlight crept across the edge of the rug like it wasn't sure it was allowed.

Annabel placed the envelope from Vera on the desk in front of him.

Grantham stared at it.

"She said she'd give it to you. In case anything happened."

He opened it slowly, reading in silence. His face didn't change — but something in his shoulders dropped.

"She knew," he said finally. "About Hale. About the forgeries. About the will."

"She told you she was making changes?"

"She said she was reviewing everything. Rafe. Juliet. The gallery."

"Did she name Juliet as heir?"

Grantham nodded. "Unofficially. The formal documents weren't signed. But the intent was clear."

Evie stepped forward. "And Hale?"

Grantham closed the envelope and set it aside.

"He's been circling Everly House for years. Buying up land. Pressuring institutions. He wanted a controlling stake in the estate."

"Why didn't Vera stop him earlier?"

"She was afraid."

He said it with no bitterness. Just fact. The kind of truth that had sat quietly in corners for years.

Annabel's gaze sharpened.

"But she wasn't afraid anymore. Not when she hid the pearls. The microfilm. The ring and key."

Grantham blinked.

"The key?"

Annabel produced it from her pocket, alongside the Everly signet ring.

Grantham paled.

His composure slipped — not a collapse, just a fraying at the edge. His hands tightened briefly, knuckles whitening.

"That key unlocks the trunk in my vault."

"And what's inside?"

"Original deeds. Proof that Vera's holdings were acquired before Hale's influence. A ledger. And... a letter."

Annabel's voice was low.

"A confession?"

"A naming. She writes that Hale was behind the death at the cliffs."

Evie drew a sharp breath.

"That was the first case," she whispered. "Your first case."

Annabel nodded.

"And we never had proof."

Grantham looked from the ring to the key.

"You do now."

Outside, a breeze moved through the hallway — and for a moment, it felt like the house exhaled.

Chapter 13

The garden was unusually quiet for midday.

Even the bees seemed reverent. Shadows dappled the stone path like lacework, and the air smelled faintly of lavender, earth, and the past.

Juliet sat on a stone bench beneath the wisteria, her posture as elegant as ever, but her gaze distant. A teacup rested beside her, untouched. The pearls of her earrings caught the sunlight in tiny, trembling flashes.

Annabel approached slowly.

"She wanted you to have it all," she said.

Juliet didn't turn. "She wanted too many things. Legacy. Peace. Revenge."

"She gave us the tools."

Juliet finally looked at her.

"But not the courage."

"She thought you had it."

Juliet gave a hollow laugh.

"She also thought I'd marry a baron and take up watercolours."

Evie appeared, holding a padded box. She opened it without ceremony.

Inside: the pearls.

They didn't gleam — they glowed. Softly. Like moonlight pooled in silk.

Juliet stared at them.

"She still had them?"

"She moved them. Re-hid them. Probably the morning of the gala. She was setting the trap."

"For Hale?"

Annabel nodded. "And for whoever might try to stop her."

Juliet's eyes filled — not tears, but some sharper emotion. Guilt. Grief. Resolve.

"She said she was done being afraid."

"She meant it," Annabel said.

Persephone padded up the path, her black fur catching no dust, her steps utterly silent. She stopped beside the bench and blinked at Juliet.

Juliet reached out — slowly — and the cat allowed a single stroke.

"She was always watching," Juliet whispered.

"She still is," Annabel said. "But now it's your turn."

Juliet took the pearls from the box.

They felt cool. Weighty. A truth worn around the throat.

"They belong to the house."

Annabel nodded.

"And you're the house now."

Above them, a petal drifted loose from the wisteria vine. It landed silently on Juliet's shoulder. She didn't brush it away.

Chapter 14

Clarissa Fairmont was drinking port in the gallery's north room, seated beneath a portrait of some long-dead Everly ancestor with too many medals and not enough chin. She looked smaller than usual. Or maybe just older.

The room was cold — not from temperature, but history. Even the velvet chairs looked judgmental.

Annabel took the chair opposite her.

"You could have told her."

Clarissa didn't flinch. "I did. She just didn't listen."

"You left the diagram where someone could find it."

"I thought it would scare her. Force her to act."

"It did," Annabel said. "Just not in the way you expected."

Clarissa sighed.

"She changed her mind. About Juliet. About everything. Said I'd had my time."

"She was right."

"I know."

Evie entered quietly, carrying a sealed envelope.

"We found this in her dresser. It was addressed to you."

Clarissa took it slowly.

Opened it.

Inside: a letter. No flourish. No farewell. Just a single sentence, written in Vera's sharp, slanting hand.

"You were never second — I just expected more from you."

Clarissa's breath hitched. Not loudly. Just enough to crack the air around her. She touched the edge of the paper like it might bruise.

"I loved her," she said.

"I know."

"She didn't love anyone."

Annabel tilted her head.

"She loved Little Firling. In her way. She loved the name. The house. The performance of legacy."

Clarissa gave a bitter smile. "And you. She admired you."

"She admired anyone who told her the truth."

Clarissa folded the letter and tucked it into her pocket.

"What now?"

"You help us finish what she started."

"Bring down Hale?"

Annabel nodded.

"You're a witness. A voice. A link to her past."

Clarissa stood slowly.

She looked taller now — not prouder, exactly, but less afraid of fading.

"I always wanted a role."

Evie smiled.

"You've got one."

Chapter 15

It came together faster than expected.

Rafe, once uncooperative, now provided access to financial records — partial, redacted, but telling. The catering contracts were traced to a non-existent branch of Plume Events. The catering van had expired plates. The driver, Liam, identified the man who had paid him in cash as "not the man's real name — but his eyes were cold."

And Vera's letter, sealed and now properly lodged with Grantham, was the final weight.

She named Rupert Hale.

Not with accusation.

But with certainty.

"He believes power is a form of inheritance," she wrote. "And so, I've taken back what was mine."

The words didn't rage. They didn't plead. They simply landed — heavy, final, unafraid.

PC Oakes arrived at the vicar's study just before lunch, holding the microfilm like it might bite.

"I've contacted the metropolitan fraud unit," he said.

Annabel nodded. "You'll need allies."

"I'll need a battering ram."

"You've got one."

She placed the ring and key on the table.

They didn't look like weapons. But Oakes took a step back all the same.

"The trunk in Grantham's vault confirms everything."

Oakes exhaled slowly.

"And you're sure this will hold up?"

Evie leaned on the windowsill.

"He's been protected for too long. But Vera laid the foundation. We're just finishing the house."

Oakes nodded.

Then turned to leave.

As he passed Persephone — seated like a gargoyle beside the tea tray — he hesitated.

She blinked at him.

Slow.

Ominous.

Like she'd judged him and found him... mostly tolerable.

Oakes straightened his collar.

And left.

***

The house was quiet.

Not peaceful. Waiting.

The kind of hush that comes before a storm — not in the sky, but in rooms where legacies are rewritten.

Juliet checked the lock on the side door.

Evie laid out the files on the drawing room table like weapons in velvet.

Annabel stood by the window.

"I didn't think it would be tonight," she said softly.

"They always come at sunset," Evie replied. "When they want to be seen."

Persephone, perched on the back of an armchair, twitched her tail once.

Then, headlights swept across the drive.

And the moment arrived.

Chapter 16

Rupert Hale arrived with no warning.

His car — sleek, black, and distinctly unsuited to Little Firling's cobbled lanes — pulled up outside Everly House just after sunset. The air inside had thickened, as if the walls themselves recognized an intruder.

He stepped out as if he owned the place. In a way, he almost did.

Annabel was waiting for him in the drawing room, Evie beside her. Juliet lingered near the fireplace, pale but steady.

Persephone sat atop the sideboard, tail curling like punctuation.

Hale didn't bother with greetings.

"I assume you think you've won."

"I don't play your game," Annabel replied. Her voice was calm, but her fingers curled tighter around the edge of the chair.

He laughed — sharp, joyless.

"Everyone plays. The difference is who knows it."

Evie stepped forward.

"Vera knew. That's why she left the letter. The evidence."

"She left paranoia."

"She left proof," Annabel said. "Deeds. Signatures. Microfilm."

Hale's jaw tightened.

"None of it holds up in court."

"But it holds up in Little Firling," Annabel said. "And in Parliament. And in the press."

Juliet spoke then — her voice clear, steady.

"You don't get to control us anymore."

Hale turned toward her, something flickering behind his eyes.

"Your aunt was always sentimental. She left you a mess."

"No," Juliet said. "She left me the house. And the truth."

Persephone stood. Her eyes, golden and gleaming, never blinked — the stare of something ancient, feline, and unimpressed.

She leapt down. Walked across the rug — and sat at Hale's feet. Looking up. Silent. Unblinking.

Hale flinched.

It was slight.

But it was enough.

And the room knew it.

Chapter 17

The arrest came three days later.

Not in the dead of night — Hale wouldn't have allowed that — but in the full glare of afternoon, with the press waiting at the bottom of the hill and Oakes standing straighter than he ever had in his life.

Forgery. Fraud. Coercion. Historical theft.

The charges read like the preface to a true crime bestseller.

Clarissa gave a statement. So did Grantham. Juliet submitted the family tree. Rafe, unexpectedly, verified the financial discrepancies. Even Liam — shaking and pale — testified by video call.

***

Annabel ran her fingers along the spines of the Everly estate records, their leather cracked like the surface of old secrets. Most volumes had been arranged with meticulous care — trust deeds, art appraisals, donation records. And yet, one folder didn't belong.

It was thinner than the others. No label on the spine. Stuffed between "Estate Expenses, 1981–1990" and "Gala Planning: Tricentennial Edition."

She pulled it out slowly.

Inside: a single torn page. Handwritten. Barely legible, but unmistakably Vera's.

"If anyone asks, he was never born here. He was never named. But if he comes back — you'll know him by the ring."

Annabel froze.

No date.

No signature.

Just a postscript, scribbled in the margin:

Don't tell Juliet. Not yet.

"Evie," she called.

Evie appeared in the doorway, holding a half-empty tin of mints. "Don't tell me we found a ghost heir."

Annabel held up the page.

"Not a ghost. But maybe a shadow."

Evie groaned. "I hate shadows. They're never straightforward."

"Neither is legacy."

Persephone, who had been curled in a window nook, opened one eye.

The look said: *Oh no, not again.*

Annabel folded the note, slid it into her pocket, and murmured, "Secrets always echo. Some just take longer to find their voice."

***

Annabel found Mrs. Gilchrist precisely where she expected: polishing the silver in the quiet of the back kitchen of Everly house at dusk, her posture as upright as the candlesticks.

"Miss Deighton," Gilchrist said without turning. "If you're here to talk about the will, I have nothing to add."

"I'm here about the ring," Annabel replied.

That made the polish cloth pause — for just a heartbeat.

"Lots of rings in this house."

"This one unlocks a vault. One Vera left behind. And a note suggesting someone else may have a claim."

Mrs. Gilchrist finally turned, her face as unreadable as the garden hedge maze.

"She never trusted banks," she said flatly. "Said the vault was only for things the living didn't know how to carry."

"And the boy?"

A silence thick enough to slice.

"She told me once," Gilchrist said slowly, "that not all debts are money. Some are names. Some are disappearances."

Annabel stepped closer.

"She hid a name."

"She *protected* one," Gilchrist corrected. "There's a difference. That boy was born under shame and silence — and Vera swore he'd never suffer for her mistakes."

"Was he Hale's?"

Gilchrist's jaw tightened. "He was hers."

No more. No less.

Annabel nodded once. "If he comes back?"

"Then you'd best pray he's nothing like his uncle."

She picked up the polish again and returned to her work.

***

Two days after the arrest, the first satellite van arrived by mid-morning.

By noon, there were six.

Little Firling, normally sleepy and floral, buzzed like a beehive poked with a boom mic.

A man in a tweed suit stood outside the bakery asking questions about "Lady Vera's last jam preference."

Three influencers filmed a #TrueCrimeWalk outside the chapel, one of them mispronouncing "Everly" four different ways.

Annabel watched from behind the lace curtain of the tea shop, sipping her blend and bracing herself.

Evie burst in, winded and indignant. "One of them just tried to interview Persephone."

Annabel didn't blink. "Is he still alive?"

"Barely. Scratched the living truth out of his forearm."

They stepped outside together.

A Daily Truth tabloid reporter attempted to corner them.

"Miss Deighton! Can you confirm the pearls were cursed? And were you romantically involved with the inspector?"

"I am," Annabel said, "deeply committed to my kettle."

They kept walking.

Behind them, Persephone strutted down the path like a general returning from battle.

Someone snapped a picture.

She growled.

The camera short-circuited.

Annabel smiled.

"Little Firling doesn't do circus," she said.

Evie adjusted her sunhat. "But it does do clean-up."

***

The pearls were recovered. Not from Hale, but from a hidden compartment in the catering van, found abandoned near a farm on the outskirts of Lincoln.

Juliet had them polished and mounted in a museum-style display in the Everly gallery.

"On loan," she told the press. "From the estate. For the people."

Persephone was given the position of unofficial gallery guardian, though she preferred the west windowsill and growled at anyone who tried to photograph her.

Annabel returned to her cottage with a new set of notes, two thank-you baskets, and the quiet satisfaction of puzzles completed.

Evie resumed her role as village archivist — part detective, part historian, full gossip.

And for the first time in weeks, Little Firling exhaled.

The spring sun softened. The garden bloomed.

And the village settled back into the hum of secrets not yet uncovered.

Epilogue

Annabel sipped her tea on the back porch, a wool shawl over her shoulders and a crossword tucked under one elbow. The crossword was only half-finished — something about birdwatching slang and obscure British biscuits — but she was more focused on the view.

The garden was humming again. Not whispering, not brooding — just humming. Birds argued in the hedges. A bee flirted with a dahlia. The world, for once, was not keeping secrets.

Evie emerged from the cottage with a box labelled "ARCHIVES — DO NOT BURN," muttering about the lack of alphabetization in the local history logs.

"Someone once filed a sea monster sighting under *Cabbages*," she announced. "We are a nation of lunatics."

Persephone sat atop the railing, tail flicking lazily, her eyes closed in a sunbeam. She was not asleep. She never slept when mysteries were afoot — only rested her eyes in judgment.

"I've been thinking," Annabel said.

Evie paused. "Oh dear."

"We should make it official."

"The podcast?"

"No, the register. A proper one. The Little Firling Puzzle Archive. A living log of all unresolved oddities, possible crimes, and curious folk tales."

"With ribbons?"

"And index cards."

Evie grinned.

Persephone stretched.

Then, with great drama, the cat turned her head toward the gate.

A postman was approaching. Not their usual one — this man walked with careful posture, as though carrying fragile secrets instead of packages.

He handed Annabel a slim parcel. No return address. Just a wax seal stamped with what looked like a brushstroke and a question mark.

Evie peered over her shoulder. "Looks like someone wants us at that art retreat after all."

Annabel opened the parcel.

Inside: a sketch. Delicate. Wild. And in one corner, half-erased — the shape of a face no one had yet named.

Persephone leapt down.

She sniffed the paper.

Then turned sharply toward the rose trellises, ears twitching.

Annabel rose.

Another whisper.

Another secret.

Another brushstroke on the canvas of Little Firling.

She turned to Evie.

"Shall we?"

Evie picked up her notebook.

Persephone trotted ahead.

And together, they stepped into the next mystery.

***

Persephone walked alone beneath the wisteria.

The village was sleeping. Humans dreamed their muddled dreams, cluttered with memory and nonsense. But the night air whispered clearer truths

— rustling leaves, distant fox prints, and the scent of change drifting in like sea fog.

She moved like ink in water.

Silent. Certain.

The Everly House loomed behind her, heavy with the echoes of what had been buried, revealed, rearranged.

She paused beneath the sundial.

Sniffed.

Something lingered in the earth there — old metal, ribbon silk, the last trace of Vera's will not yet read.

Persephone sat. Watched. Waited.

From across the fields, wind tugged at the hedgerows. Somewhere, an owl called — low and warning.

Persephone did not answer.

She was not prey.

She was the watcher between worlds. Between candlelight and clue. Between tea trays and truths.

Tomorrow, the humans would return to routines.

Annabel would misplace her reading glasses again. Evie would mutter about poor filing systems. The kettle would whistle. The archive would yawn.

But something else was coming.

The cat could feel it.

A ripple beneath the rose trellis. A sketch left unfinished. A lie whispered in turpentine.

Persephone rose.

She turned toward the east, where the morning would rise behind the hills, and walked — not hurried, not hunting, just *ready.*

Because peace was only a pause.

And someone would soon forget that Little Firling remembers everything.

Especially the cat.